ABOUT THE BANK STREET READY-TO-READ SERIES

Seventy years of educational research and innovative teaching have given the Bank Street College of Education the reputation as America's most trusted name in early childhood education.

Because no two children are exactly alike in their development, we have designed the *Bank Street Ready-to-Read* series in three levels to accommodate the individual stages of reading readiness of children ages four through eight.

- *Level 1:* GETTING READY TO READ—read-alouds for children who are taking their first steps toward reading.

- *Level 2:* READING TOGETHER—for children who are just beginning to read by themselves but may need a little help.

- *Level 3:* I CAN READ IT MYSELF—for children who can read independently.

Our three levels make it easy to select the books most appropriate for a child's development and enable him or her to grow with the series step by step. The *Bank Street Ready-to-Read* books also overlap and reinforce each other, further encouraging the reading process.

We feel that making reading fun and enjoyable is the single most important thing that you can do to help children become good readers. And we hope you'll be a part of Bank Street's long tradition of learning through sharing.

The Bank Street College of Education

To Jonathan Matthew Davies
—W.H.H.

For Kitty
—D.C.

FEED ME!

A Bantam Little Rooster Book/November 1992

Little Rooster is a trademark of Bantam Books,
a division of Bantam Doubleday Dell Publishing Group, Inc.

Series graphic design by Alex Jay/Studio J

Special thanks to James A. Levine, Betsy Gould,
and Diane Arico.

Library of Congress Cataloging-in-Publication Data

Hooks, William H.
Feed me! : an Aesop fable / retold by William H. Hooks ;
illustrated by Doug Cushman.
p. cm.—(Bank Street ready-to-read)
Adaptation of: The lark in the cornfield.
"A Byron Preiss book."
"A Bantam little rooster book."
Summary: A mother lark whose nest in the farmer's corn
is threatened by the coming harvest uses wisdom
in deciding when to move her babies.
ISBN 0-553-08950-1.—ISBN 0-553-37023-5 (pbk.)
[1. Fables.] I. Aesop. II. Cushman, Doug, ill.
III. Lark in the cornfield. IV. Title. V. Series.
PZ8.2.H64Fe 1992
398.24'58812—dc20
91-40275 CIP AC

Published simultaneously in the United States and Canada

PRINTED IN THE UNITED STATES OF AMERICA

0 9 8 7 6 5 4 3 2 1

Bank Street Ready-to-Read™

Feed Me!
An Aesop Fable

Retold by William H. Hooks
Illustrated by Doug Cushman

A Byron Preiss Book

A BANTAM LITTLE ROOSTER BOOK
NEW YORK · TORONTO · LONDON · SYDNEY · AUCKLAND

A mother lark made a nest
in a cornfield.
She laid four beautiful eggs.

"Soon I'll have
four beautiful babies,"
she said.
And soon she did.

As the corn grew,
so did the babies.
They were always hungry.
The mother lark spent all day
looking for food.

Whenever the babies saw her
they chirped . . .

7

The corn grew tall
and the baby birds grew big.
They chirped
louder than ever...

The mother lark began
to worry.
Soon the corn would be ripe.
The farmer would come
to cut it.
What would become
of her babies?

"Watch for the farmer,"
the mother bird said
to her babies.
The babies said...

"Listen to the farmer,"
she warned.
The babies said...

"Tell me everything you hear," said the mother bird.
The babies chirped...

So the mother lark flew away to look for food.

When she came home
the babies were very hungry.
They chirped...

The mother bird said,
"First, tell me:
Did you watch for the farmer?"
The babies chirped...

Then they all said together...

"Wait!" said the mother lark.
"Did you listen?
What did the farmer say?"
The baby birds cried...

15

"There is no need to be scared,"
said the mother lark.
"Neighbors are not so quick
to cut corn for someone else."
Then she fed her hungry babies.

The next day the mother lark
flew off again for food.
"Watch, listen, and
tell me everything,"
she said.

When she returned to the nest, the babies were hiding.
"It is only me," said the lark.
"What did you see today?"

The babies cried...

Then they all
chirped together…

"Wait," said the mother lark.
"Tell me what you heard."
The babies chirped...

21

"Don't worry," said the mother.
"Friends will be slow to come
and cut the corn."
Then she fed
her hungry babies.

The next day the mother lark
came home early
with fat worms
for the baby birds.
The babies cried...

"Not yet," said the mother lark.
"What did you see today?"

"What did you hear?"
asked the mother lark.
The babies cried...

The mother lark
looked worried.
The babies cried...

"Eat quickly!"
said the mother lark.
"Tonight we will move.
When people do
their own work,
things get done."

So the mother lark
moved her babies
to the woods
that very night.

William H. Hooks is the author of many books for children, including the highly acclaimed *Moss Gown* and, most recently, *The Three Little Pigs and the Fox.* He currently lives in Chapel Hill, North Carolina.

Doug Cushman is the author and illustrator of many children's books, including *Possum Stew, Camp Big Paw,* and *Aunt Eater Loves a Mystery,* a *Reading Rainbow* selection. He has most recently illustrated the Bank Street Ready-to-Read title *How Do You Make a Bubble?* Mr. Cushman lives in New Haven, Connecticut, with his wife, illustrator Kim Mulkey.

DATE			